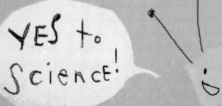

When
You've
had
ENOUGH
of
BiG gies
and MaDdies
and MEAN ies
and BULLies
and BADdies
and GRaBbies
and Fools
and

Wee Rebel
books
also by
John & Jana

A Rule Is To Break:
A Child's Guide to Anarchy

Happy Punks 1 2 3:
A Counting Story

Gorilla Gardener:
How to Help Nature Take Over the World

We Say NO! ©2017 by John Seven & Jana Christy
All rights reserved. ISBN 978-1-945665-06-6
Published by Manic D Press. For information, contact
Manic D Press, PO Box 410804, San Francisco CA 94141
www.manicdpress.com
Printed in the USA   CPSAI compliant

You THINK!

OP!

and make

LoTS OF MiS

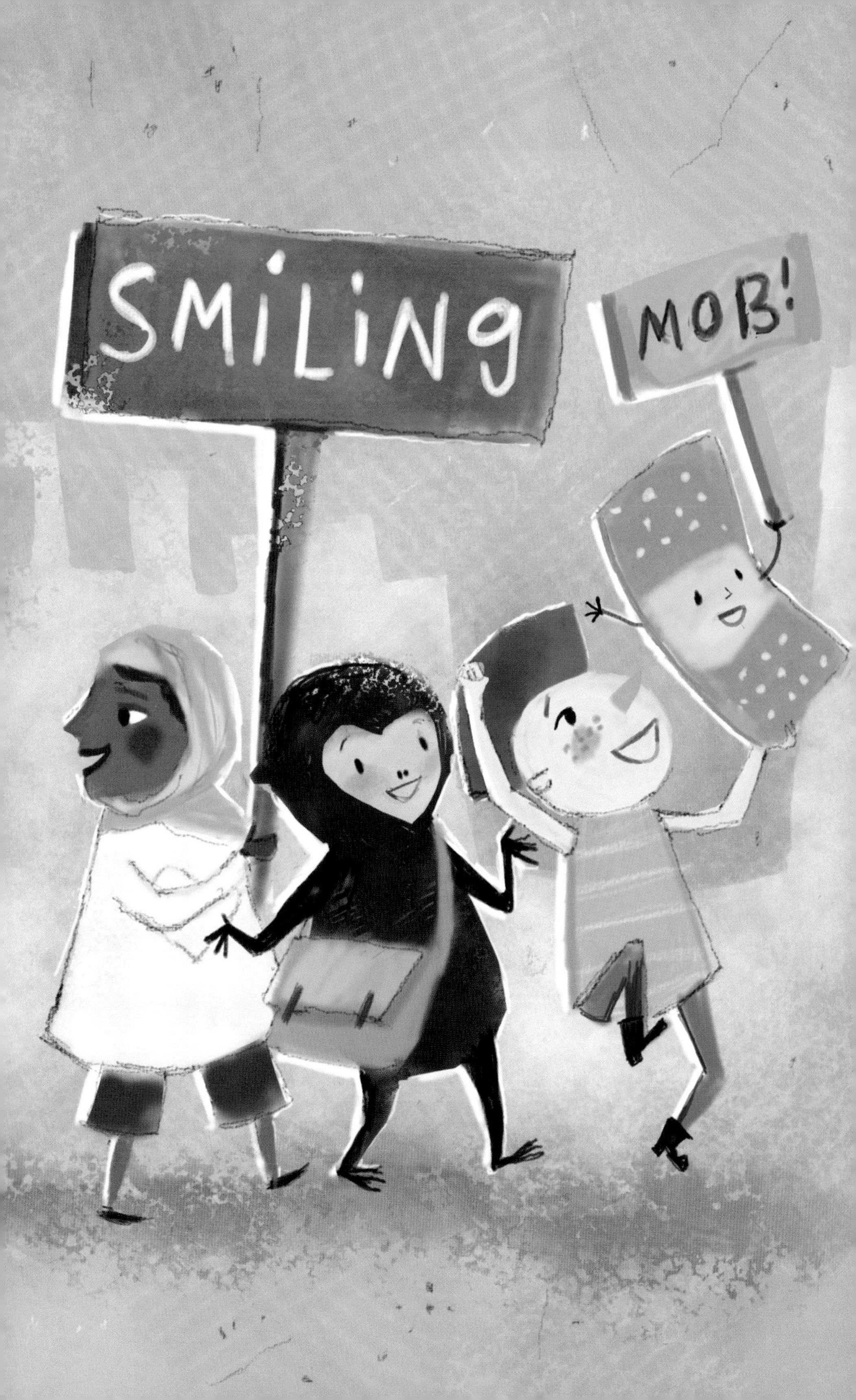
SMILING
MOB!

If they build a statue

Fix it.

WHEn They TRY to SeLL you SOmethiNg...

No.

N. O.

(you know what to do.)

DiffeRence

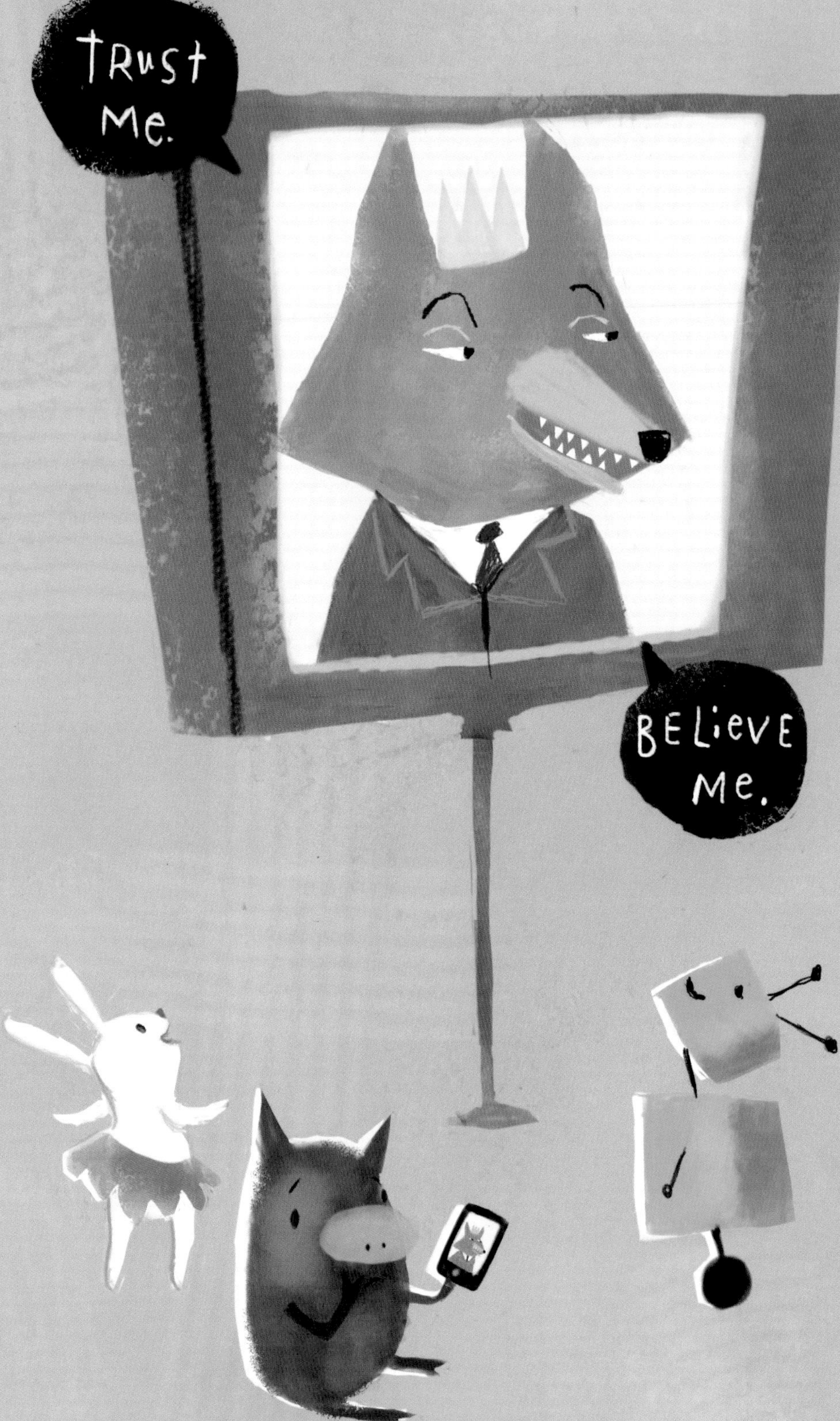
TRUST ME.
BELIEVE ME.

Don't BE FOOLED.

I wouldn't necessarily BeLieve him

If something
gets taken,

take it

BACK.

Leave
Heaps of spaghetti!
Knock knock! Who's there? Canoe! Canoe who? Canoe come over and play?
Smell a Flower
I'll Be YOUR
Don't forget to Listen to the Birds today!
Hi pal!
If I had a pet I would name
Nice Hair!
SUGAR is sweet and so ARE you!
would you like to dance?

SMILEY-NOTES

EVERYWHERE!

Resistance shouldn't be boring-

Have fun!

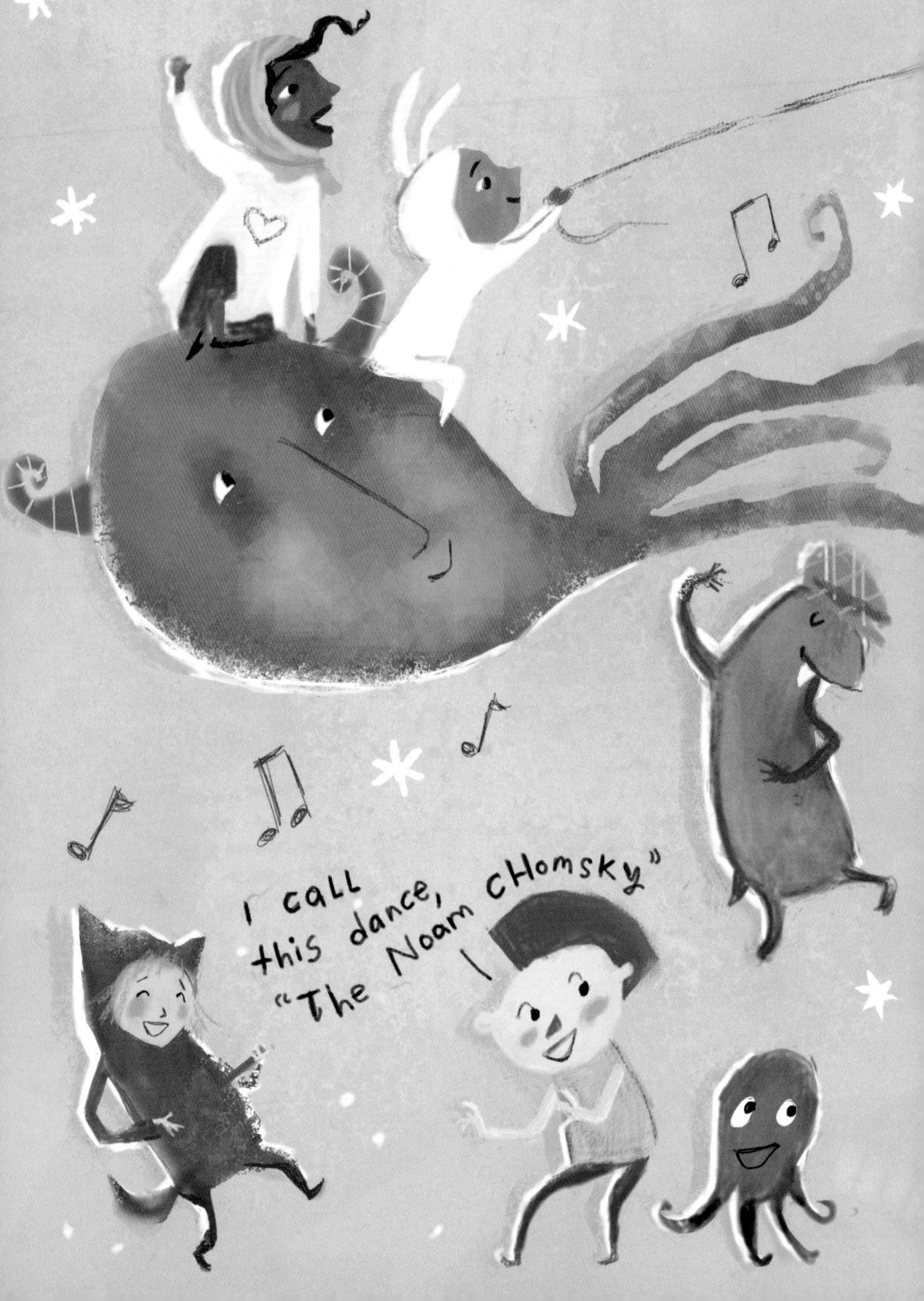

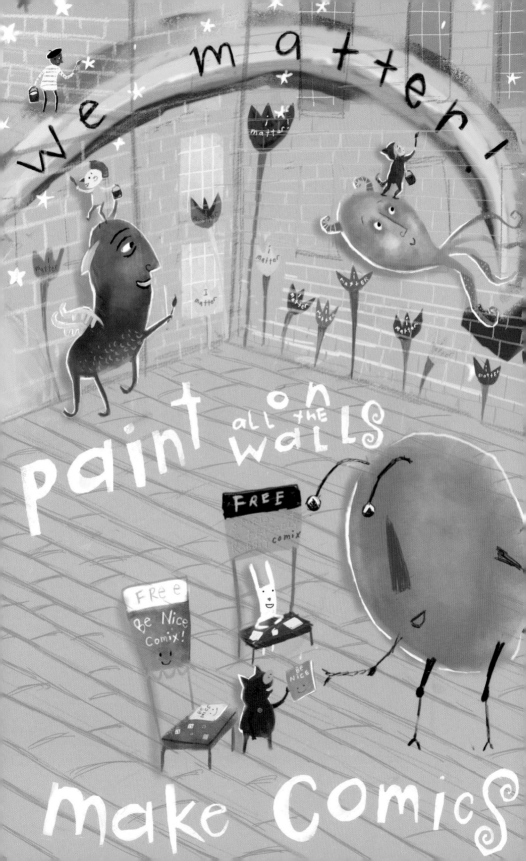

If they

01101100 01100101
Find a new way to communicate!
01101100 01100101
01110011 01110100

If th^ey p^e ek

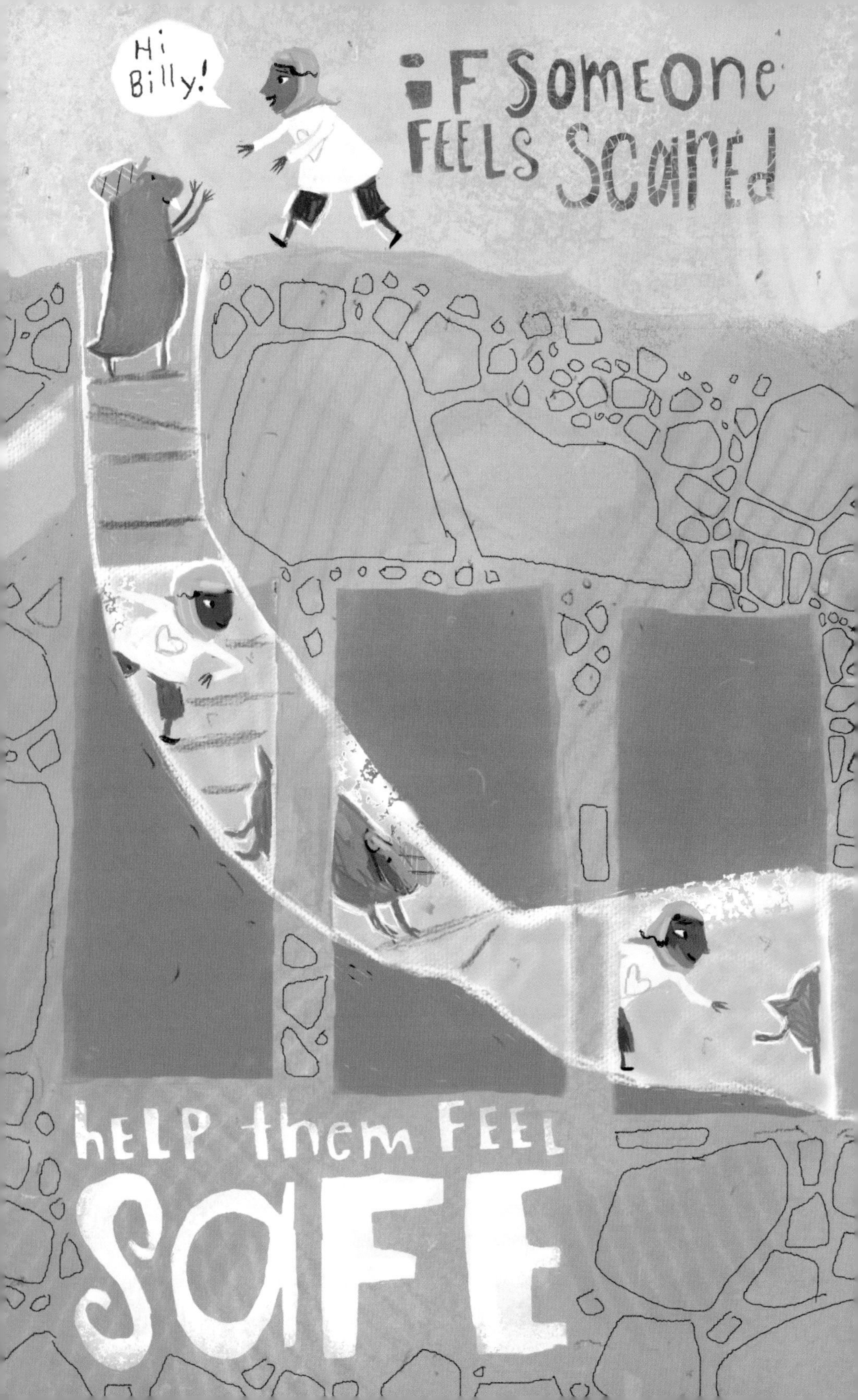

IF SOMEONE FEELS SCARED

HELP THEM FEEL SAFE

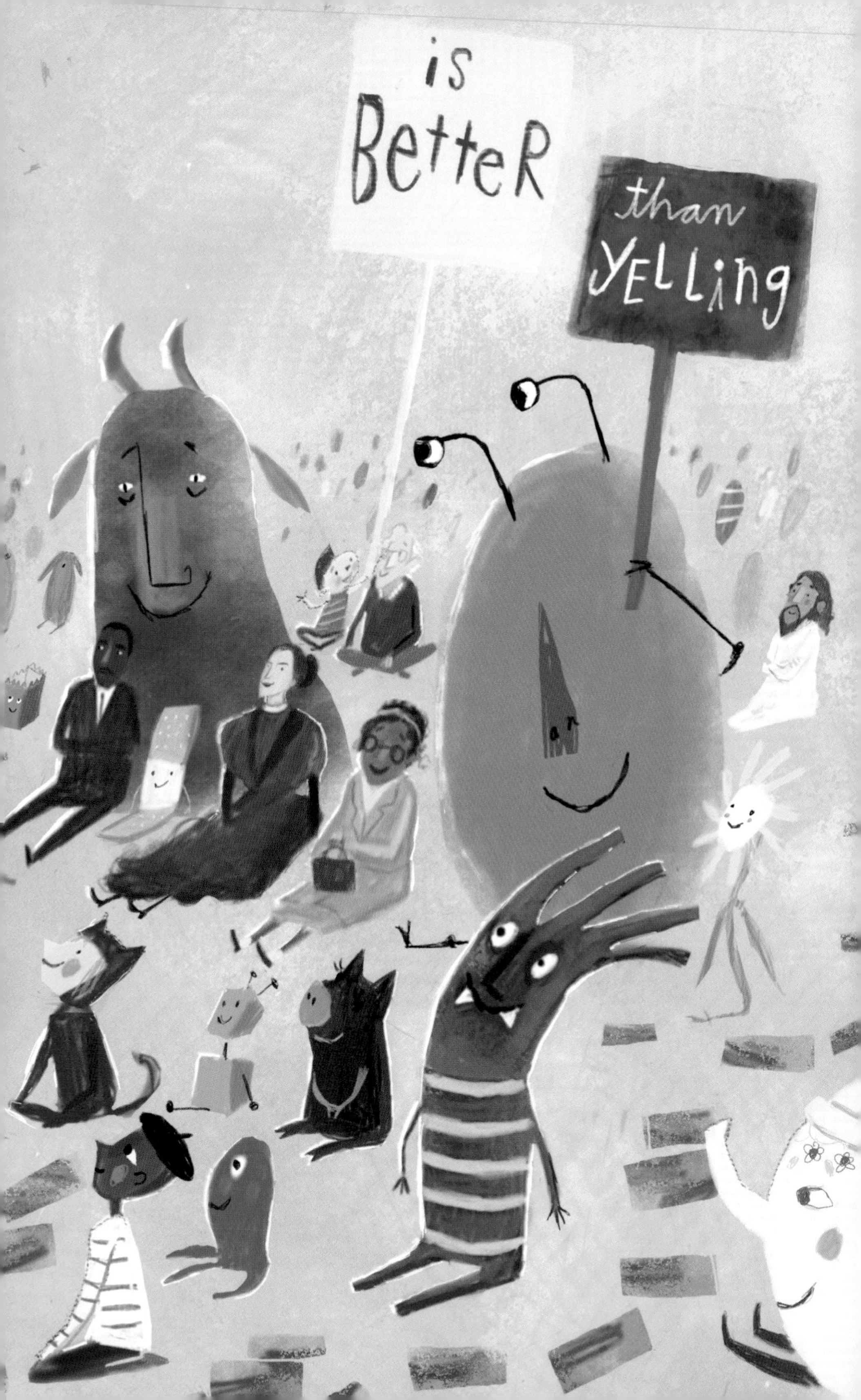
is
BetteR
than
YELLing

And remember

the
REVOLUtion
is
OVER

ONLY
WHEN

A Note FroM jOhn & jana!

SOMETiMES people don't act very fairly.

And sometimes the people in charge won't do anything about it. It might even be the people in charge who don't act fairly. Maybe they act like bullies! You tried talking and asking nicely, but that didn't work. When that happens you have to take care of things yourself.

> You can practice Resistance.
> You can even have a Revolution.

Resistance means to take action against the people who aren't acting fairly. Revolution means to change things. If something is not right, you can have a revolution to stop it. There is no one way to have a revolution and you can have a revolution a bunch of different ways at once.

The most popular kind of revolution is when people march down streets in a big crowd, carrying signs and making sure the people in charge know what the ordinary people want.

The very best kind of revolution is one where people don't get hurt.

Whatever kind of resistance you choose and whichever revolution you decide to be part of, we hope it is part of an effort to make the world a better place,

because the world can always be better than it is.